BABY CHRISTMAS

Michael Lawrence

Illustrated by
Arthur Robins

ORCHARD BOOKS

IT WAS Christmas Eve, and there were lots of presents to deliver down lots of chimneys. But when Father Christmas put on his Christmas suit, Baby Christmas began to cry.

'Oh dear,' said Mother Christmas.

'Oh dear,
oh dear,
oh deary-me.
What can
we do to
cheer you up?'

To keep Baby Christmas amused,
Mother Christmas dressed him up in
his Baby Christmas suit and sat him
in his Baby Christmas sleigh.
She even gave him a sack of toys
to pretend to deliver.

'There! Now
you're just like
Father!'

But then . . .

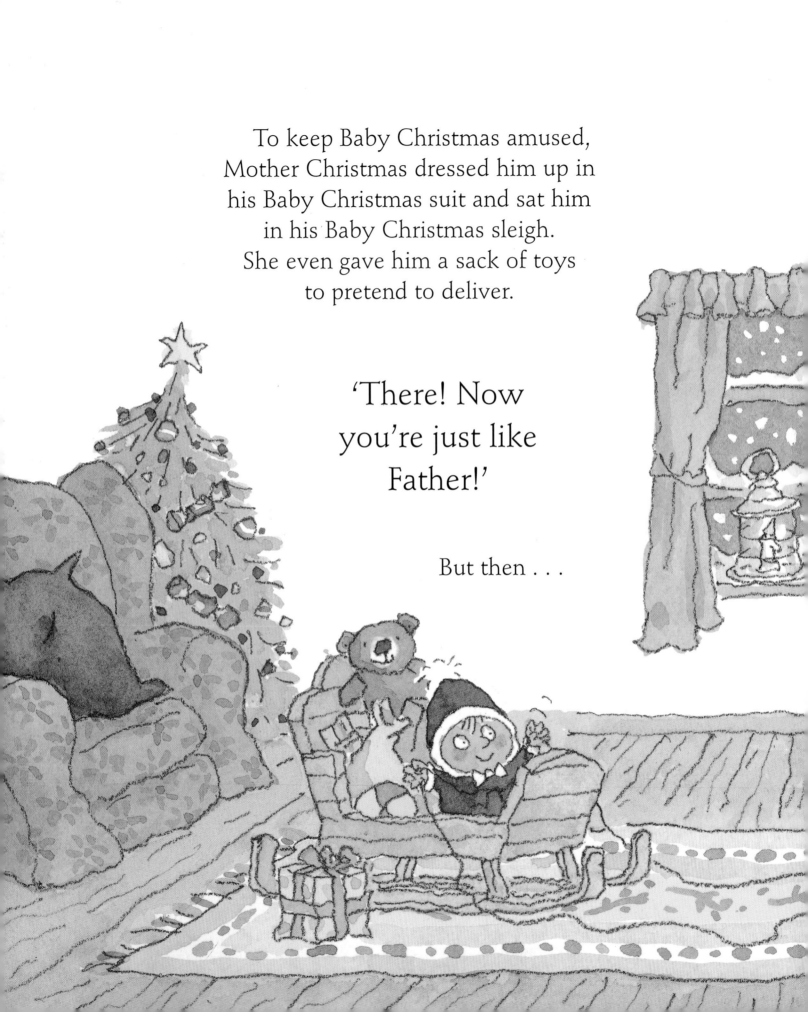

'My mince pies!'
Mother Christmas cried.
And away she went to rescue them
before they burnt to
a frizzle,

a frazzle,

a fruppety-froo.

While Mother Christmas was gone another nose began to twitch.

'Nun-nun-nun-nooooooose!'

said Baby Christmas.

Rudolf Junior's nose had never glowed before, but he knew what it meant.

It meant that he was old enough to fly!

'Ho-ho,'
said Baby Christmas.

'Wa-heee,' said he,
as out they flew into
the dark and frosty night.

Father Christmas was just about to set off on his rounds when Mother Christmas missed her little one.

Mother and Father Christmas searched **high** and **low**

and low and high
for their little lost lad.

Where could he be?

Where could
he **be**?

Where **could** he be?

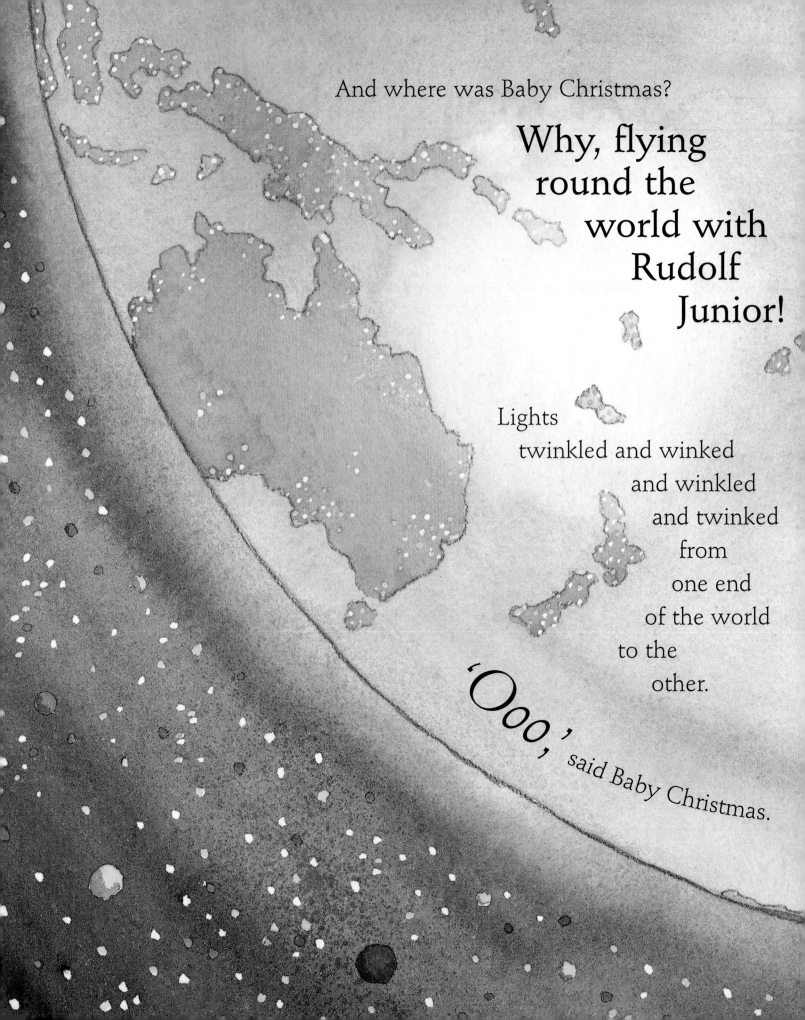

And where was Baby Christmas?

Why, flying round the world with Rudolf Junior!

Lights twinkled and winked and winkled and twinked from one end of the world to the other.

'Ooo,' said Baby Christmas.

Down they went, and up again, and round...

...and round and round and round again,

...until they were quite, quite giddy. 'Wheeee!' cried Baby Christmas.

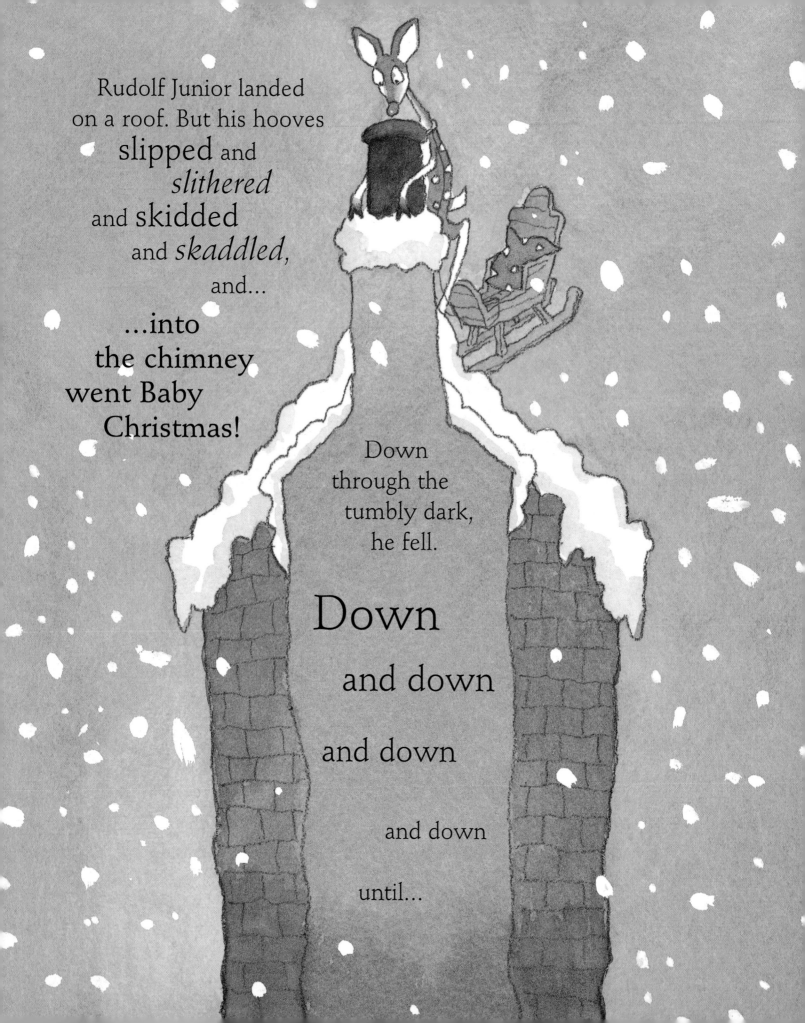

Rudolf Junior landed
on a roof. But his hooves
slipped and
slithered
and skidded
and *skaddled,*
and...

...into
the chimney
went Baby
Christmas!

Down
through the
tumbly dark,
he fell.

Down
and down

and down

and down

until...

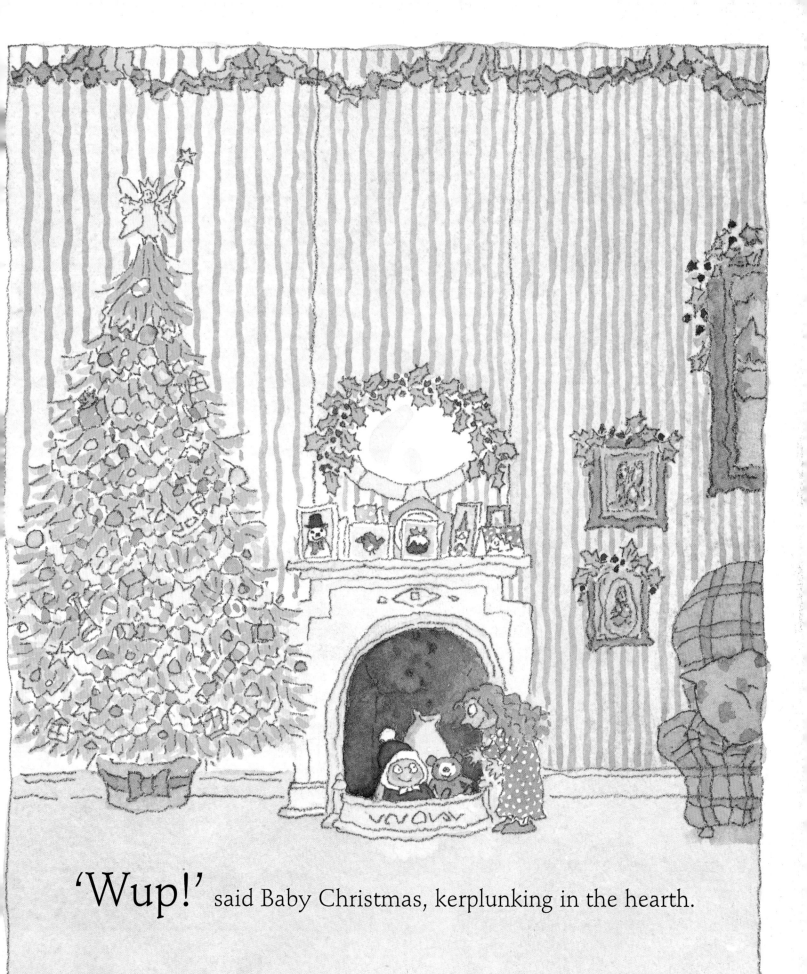

'Wup!' said Baby Christmas, kerplunking in the hearth.

Mother and
Father Christmas had
searched and searched and
searched for Baby Christmas.

'I want my
bay-hay-hay-
haaay-bee!'

Mother Christmas wailed.

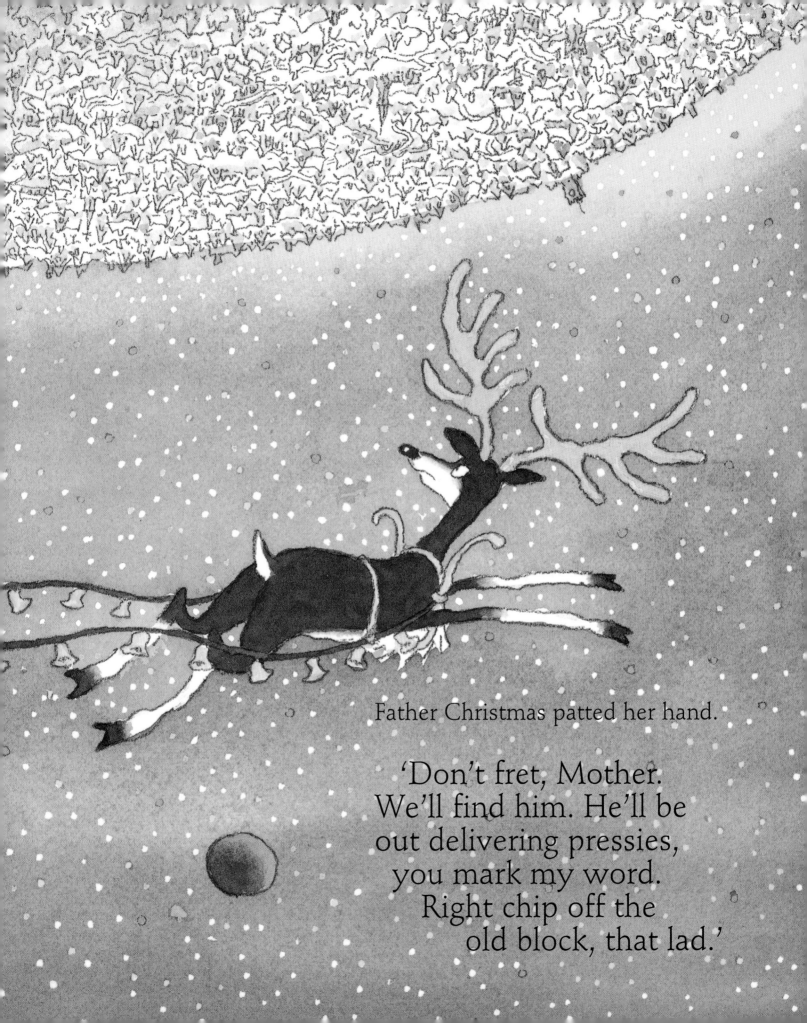

Father Christmas patted her hand.

'Don't fret, Mother.
We'll find him. He'll be
out delivering pressies,
you mark my word.
Right chip off the
old block, that lad.'

In the house, far below,
Baby Christmas stared at
the big bright tree,

with its lights...

...and tinsel

...and
silver bells.

Then he
remembered
what Father
did.

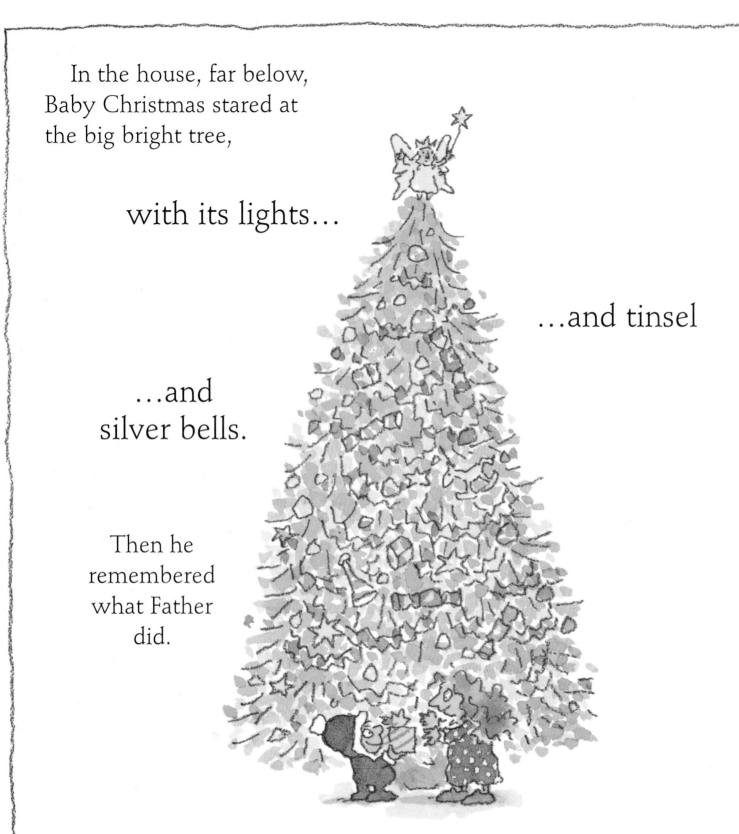

'Yappy Kissmus,' said Baby Christmas.

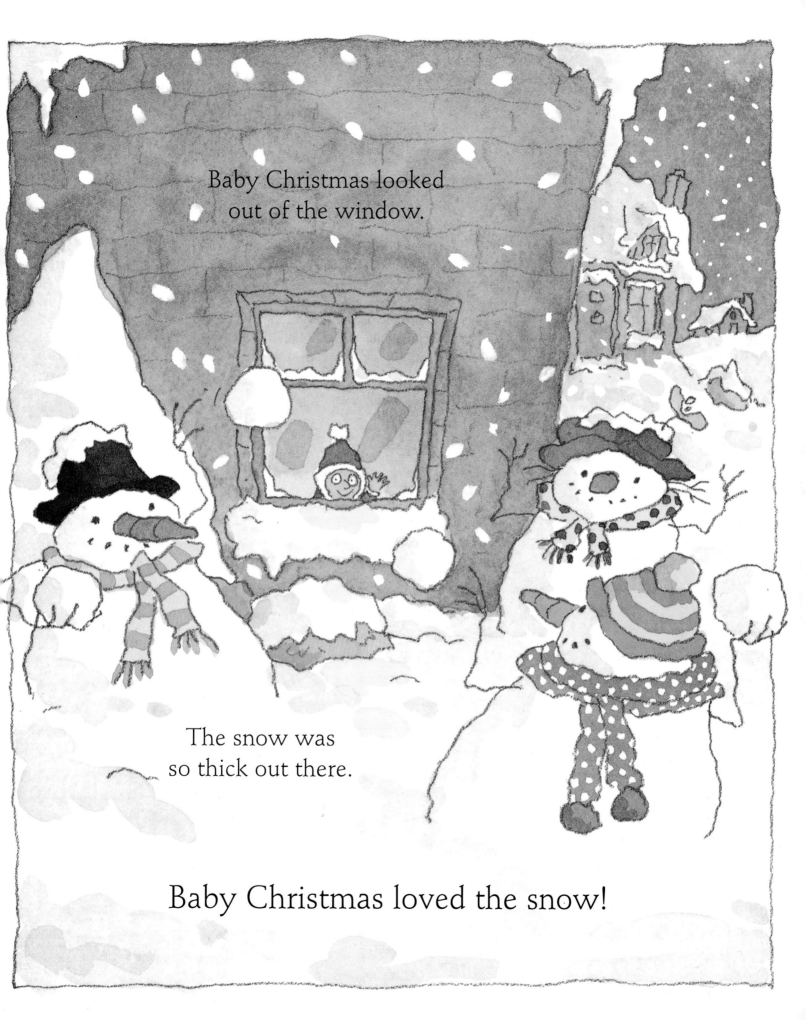

Baby Christmas looked
out of the window.

The snow was
so thick out there.

Baby Christmas loved the snow!

Suddenly Rudolf Senior
spied a small red glow,
far, far below.

He'd know that nose
anywhere!

Mother and Father
Christmas ran round
and round the garden,
as flustered as custard,
as puffed as pastry.

No sign of Baby Christmas!

But **now** they saw him!
And what a fuss they made
of him. They picked him
up and hugged him tight,
and smothered him with
Christmas kisses.

But Father had to get on.
It was the busiest night of
the year.
　　　　All those presents
to deliver, and he hadn't
even started!

Up,
they climbed,
　　and up
and up
　and up,
into the
dark and
　　frosty sky.

But as they were nearing home,

Rudolf Junior sneezed.

Aaa–
aaaa–
choooo!

And when he sneezed he lost his balance.

And when he lost his balance...

...his bright red nose took him in another direction entirely.

'Oh no!' cried Mother Christmas. 'Not again!'

After the little sleigh went
Mother and Father Christmas.
And as they went, a single
sound rang out in the dark
and frosty night.

A bubbly little sound.

A very Christmassy little sound.

A tinselly little sound.

Baby Christmas laughing!